JOSEPHINE DAUDRY

Kevin Bailey

JOSEPHINE DAUDRY

iUniverse books may be ordered through booksellers or by contacting:

iUniverse
1663 Liberty Drive
Bloomington, IN 47403
www.iuniverse.com
844-349-9409

Because of the dynamic nature of the Internet, any web addresses or links contained in this book may have changed since publication and may no longer be valid. The views expressed in this work are solely those of the author and do not necessarily reflect the views of the publisher, and the publisher hereby disclaims any responsibility for them.

Any people depicted in stock imagery provided by Getty Images are models, and such images are being used for illustrative purposes only.
Certain stock imagery © Getty Images.

ISBN: 978-1-6632-5196-1 (sc)
ISBN: 978-1-6632-5197-8 (e)

Library of Congress Control Number: 2023910320

Print information available on the last page.

iUniverse rev. date: 06/05/2023

CONTENTS

INTRODUCTION

About thirty years ago my wife and I, being recently married, each with two children of our own; were visiting a friends camp in the Adirondacks and there were two family names burnished onto wooden signs on the camp porch; Lacey and MacClean. Those names always have stuck with me...because the oldest of our girls, being a teenager at the time, was saying, "I hate my name and want to change it!" I saw the signs on the camp as we drove in the driveway and replied, "There you go...see those signs? That would be a cool name...Lacey MacClean." Her reply was "Hmph" and a shrug. She grew out of that desire, but ever since that day I have always wanted to write a song, a poem or a story where that was the name of a woman character. So after all this time, here is my attempt, I hope you enjoy it.

AUTHOR'S NOTE

*E*veryone effects the lives of those close to them and many who they may never know. A simple act of kindness or meanness will weave its way into the fabric of societal life. Those who have affected my life and the lives of my family have made this book possible. Some brought traumas, others, healing. But through it all, the love and understanding we can share as human beings carries us forward. For all who take time to listen…this story is a big 'Thank you.' It is also a celebration of life, family and nature. Taking the time to recognize and celebrate this life is the only way to truly live it. This story is a part of that celebration for me.

ACKNOWLEDGEMENTS

I would like to thank all those who had input into this story directly or indirectly. My wife, Linda, for her medical knowledge and loving support, as well as that of our children. My sister and author Rochelle Hamel for her help and editorial skills. It was her book of short stories, *The Road Less Traveled* that gave me the inspiration to start writing this novella. Thank you to the iUniverse team, and my sister Deborah Owens for their editorial help as well.

A special thank you to the guys at Morey's Diner, especially Chris, for the auto tech advice, and to all who read my first draft and gave me encouragement and pointers to complete this final version.

Finally, I thank Jesus of Nazareth. His teachings and my relationship to him have made my life what it is. As a retired pastor, I am thankful for all the lives I have been able to be a part of. The church folks I have in my life have been such an encouragement to me. Also the folks from NBSI (Network of Biblical Storytellers International), have had such a positive impact on my faith life, and I am thankful to them. And lastly to the Divine Artist who paints the sky everyday…I am so very grateful.

Kevin Bailey

1

'LACEY' AND THE D.M.V.

*J*osephine Daudry, a thirty-two year old single woman, sits by her window with pen and pad jotting down names while nursing a cup of coffee. She is tired of her name, and her situation in life. She jots down names, and crosses them off until she hits on this one, *Lacey MacClean*. She speaks the name out loud a few times and then muses about it.

Lacey MacClean, that's a good name. A good name for a superhero who lives incognito like, say....oh yes, Wonder Woman. By day she is a TV news anchor and by night she fights crime. Of course the only problem with being a superhero like Wonder Woman, is all the lies...the secrets. Not to mention Wonder Woman's dual love interests with her secret identity beau and her superhero boyfriend. So...complicated. So maybe Lacey is a cop, or an FBI agent or even CIA. Forget that...so many more lies in that profession. So then maybe she's none of those. How about...a tennis star? Nahh...sports are too....ahh, just too....

Josephine is very opinionated about sports culture. It was in middle school where she learned she was not fast enough or skilled enough to be picked in the first 3 for any sport. She liked sports, but not the sport culture. She wondered why winning seemed to be the only goal? She sips her coffee and thinks, *Why not celebrate the pure joy of sport itself. Oh, that book talks about the 'love of the game,' but really, who cares about that as much as they do winning. If you win, everything is good...if you lose, well, the only redemption is to get up and try again. It's like, until you win, your abilities are worthless. Who remembers the losing team, no matter how well they played. Aah...it's just...too...*"

Now Josephine has been called Josy since the early 70's, and yes, it is spelled that way. She got that nick name while working for her mom and dad at the gas station they owned. When they got her a work shirt for the gas station, her name was spelled with a 'y' instead of an 'ie'. Her dad blamed the print shop...her mom blamed her dad...but they weren't going to spend the money to get it fixed. And it became kinda cool... it was different and customers always had a comment or two about the spelling. Josy would gab with them, she was good with people, especially older folks. So Josy just kept spelling it that way at school or anywhere else and really, she really didn't like her full name, 'Josephine,' anyway.

Now, back to sports...when Josy played ping-pong or volleyball in gym class, she didn't mind if she lost because it was for the exercise and knowledge of being physically fit, and there wasn't pressure to win. Just do your best. And what she really liked was a good game, fast paced, close in score win or lose.

But then came track. She tried the high jump, and seemed to be made for it. She could run slow at the start and then gauge her speed by the height of the bar and then let herself fly while turning her body to slip over the bar. That was fun. No one to beat but the bar. She was good and the coach took notice. She practiced hard and was anxiously awaiting her first track meet. Other girls and boys took note of her ability and she started to enjoy a little bit of notoriety.

The day came for the first meet. It was in a town only a short drive from home, so her parents were there. She wasn't scared. Josy was ready. She went for her first jump...that's when it happened. There was a slight dip in the asphalt runway...she didn't see it and when she put her weight down on that leg, at full speed...crack! Josy never got to jump. It was her first meet, and her first jump, in front of her parents and the whole team, and she broke her right ankle on the runway. It was a bad break and her whole foot became swollen and all kinds of ugly colors; and then, there was the cast on for months...and what seemed like an endless rehab. Walking with crutches in school gave her a notoriety she did not want. Sympathy was for someone else...not for Josy. She decided that was it for track. She painted her cast a deep red as a vow for no more school sports.

Josy, takes another sip of coffee and looks again at the name she jotted down and thinks...*Lacey MacClean, she has deep red hair...and blue/green eyes that see right through you. And she is intensely stubborn and daring...it's in her Highland blood, after all, the clan MacClean were some of the fiercest Scots ever.* Josy likes reading historical novels about Scotland and Ireland.

Josy continues her thoughts, *Lacey is bright witted, sometimes sarcastic and then empathetic...when it suits her. She drives 'low and slow' until it's time to go 'low and fast'....and then don't get in her way. But she is mostly a joyful driver taking every drive as a journey to something new...even if it's a trip to the grocery store. Lacey knows how to enjoy life and give it her all. Aah... Lacey MacClean...that is a good name.*

Josy then thinks about her own name. *Josephine Daudry....what a dull name. A name to make fun of.* She has experienced this with her neighbor. Because whenever she goes to the laundry mat...and he sees her, he says, "Hey Ms. Daudry, going to do your 'laudry' eh? Intentionally leaving out the 'n' and then he laughs as he walks away. But he is totally unaware that she is popping his head like a pimple with her thumb and index finger. She is glad she saw that "Kids in the Hall" skit. It has saved her stress levels from getting too high many a time and is much better than the 'bang head here' experience, which hurts...and is no where near as fun as popping heads.

Josy keeps pondering about this name, *Lacey MacClean*. She doesn't know where it came from except all the Celtic novels and books she's read. *It must have been a name of one of the characters or a combo of them,* she thinks. Josy daydreams about becoming this incredible woman. *No more dull name, dull hair and dull eyes for me, and no more old 1980 Pinto wagon. A vintage Shelby GT...now that's a car for Lacey MacClean.*

Josy knows cars. She could tell the make and model of most cars from the late 60's through the 70's just by a taillight, or the steering wheel. After all, she worked at her mom and dad's gas station pumping gas and changing oil since she was 11. But then the business went bust in the late 70's and by then she was graduating from high school with no clue as to what was next.

Josy hates not knowing. While all her classmates were off to college, Josy was in limbo. Her parents were not in a good place financially after the business failed. The gas station was also their home, as the building included an apartment. So, leaving there, they found a small apartment on 'the other side of the tracks.' It was not easy for them in those days.

Josy had been working at a local diner as well as the gas station plus school. She was used to being busy. Now, as her co-workers from high school moved forward with the rest of their young adult lives, she stayed on at the diner. She had looked at colleges, but could not commit to any because she didn't know if she could afford it with her parents loss of the business. With no school or the gas station, she had too much time to think and worry. She just did not know what was coming or when.

Anticipation has always been Josy's weakness. Not knowing just makes it that much worse. Like when her mom went to the hospital for tests and no one told her anything because she was too young. She felt at 10 years old she was old enough, but no one else did. Waiting and not knowing was horrible. And the next year of her young life was hard as her mom underwent chemo and radiation. That's why she began helping out at the gas station because her mom just could not keep up with things being so tired all the time. Josy's mom got through the cancer treatments and was in remission. But for how long?

Not knowing.... it is not Josy's favorite. Like when she was waiting for her road test to get her license. The appointments were canceled and then would be rescheduled as soon as possible by the tester, who was out due to a family emergency; and in her small town there was only one tester. So it was not knowing, again, although not as serious as her mom's cancer, but still for a 16 year old, pretty important.

She couldn't wait to drive on her own. She loved cars and wanted to be in some kind of business that would keep her involved. Not a gas station, but something...maybe auto design. That took a good education which cost a lot of money. Where would she end up? She hated not knowing.

Josy finally quit working at the diner. She left there to begin working at the D.M.V., but, she is not happy there. Still sitting by her window, she looks out at the traffic passing by her apartment and thinks, *Aagh! The Department of Motor Vehicles! Everyone hates the D.M.V.* And why?

Well, first off, there is a sign on the back wall that hangs off kilter... printed on it are the three rules of the D.M.V., "Answers - $1.00, Correct Answers - $2.00, Dumb Looks - Free." Second, it is the waiting...the slow lines. Josy, from her work counter, has watched the morning bodies pile up at the door like a multi-car accident in very slow motion. She can always feel their absolute dread as they wait to be treated to an even longer wait in the blue line or the red line. And of course, she has taken a bit of pleasure telling them that they have filled out the wrong form. "Do not pass Go"...she murmurs to herself with a slight smirk, as she sends them to the forms table to start the whole process again.

'Pushing plates', as she calls her job, was obviously not her choice in a career path; but, when you have no specific plans, others will find some for you. As with many things in her life she can blame a friend for getting her to take an exam that led her to this job. A job with security, decent pay and a retirement plan. But her only response to the D.M.V. after 10 years is a long wanting sigh. And it is depressing at work to hear herself voice, for the millionth time, the profoundly helpless word of her existence there..."Next."

Lacey would never go to the D.M.V., she would have assistants to do that stuff. She would be off...off...somewhere, but where? Josy takes a sip of her coffee as she contemplates who Lacey is. The cars on the street below her apartment continue zipping along on their early morning drive. *Ahh...of course! Racing! That's who Lacey MacClean is....a Formula One driver! Not easy to get a ride in F1 as a woman. Few have done it...but hey, this is Lacey MacClean, she could just as easily be a superhero...so there!* She continues to ponder. *And who does Lacey get a ride with? McLaren of course! Aah, McLaren, another good and ancient Scottish clan name.*

Josy thinks about her last name. *Daudry...what kind of name is that? A mix of French and English.* Josy's ancestors immigrated from England to Canada and then down to Western New York. Josy thinks about where she lives. *The best thing about living here in Western New York is the race tracks, both cars and horses; and don't forget the beef on weck* (a kummelweck roll dipped in au jus and with slow cooked roast beef and a dash of horseradish) *...mmmm, so yummy!. Fast cars, fast horses and good eating.*

Josy loves going fast herself. Once, she got a ride in a Corvette! The owner, Mr. Corley, had just got a tune-up at her mom and dad's garage and offered her a ride around the block. He and his wife were family friends. They would hang out with her mom and dad on weekends sometimes. Josy excitedly asked her dad and he said yes. Her mom just shook her head. Around the block meant going from 0 to 100 mph by the end of the hill leading up to the light. It was an eighth mile and they made it in no time.

"Wow, that was fun!" She exclaimed.

"Don't tell your mom how fast we went, or she'll have my hide!" he said as he let her off back at the gas station.

Josy loved that ride. Hitting 100 mph was exhilarating. But these days her 1980 Pinto wagon can only manage about 68 mph on a good day. She has money saved for a new car...but it's not enough for what she really wants...that Shelby Mustang GT. Growing up in her early adult life with little money has made her very tight with her spending. *Besides where would I go with that kind of car?* But then she says to herself out loud, "Who cares! Anywhere with an open road." Then, she sighs and thinks, *How long will it take for me to save up that much money? By then I won't want to drive fast.*

Josy stares out her window at the sun coming through the trees with that same cup of coffee in her hand and sighs. She does that a lot... sighing. There is a longing that she can't quite grasp and wonders if she will ever be as free as the birds out the window just dancing on the wind. *Hmm...the music of the wind. What is the music I could dance to?* She wonders. And then wonders how her imaginary Lacey MacClean got to where she is in life. *What made her free to dance? Something allowed her to have confidence. But me? I am certainly not confident and certainly not free*, she thinks in a moment of clarity.

Josy can, at times, be negative, and does not like getting older. *I'm almost 33! She thinks. A third of my life is over, and what have I done? Lacey, by this age has done it all, seen it all, and is still at the top of her game. She not only races Formula One cars but in the off season loves dirt track as well. Sliding around the corners with the back end just about losing it...that's fun.*

Josy has never got into local dirt track racing. She would like to, but there always seems to be something that holds her back.

Maybe it is fear...for sure, fear has always been a driving force in Josy's life. Picked on when she was young for being tall and gangly made her fearful and shy. And then, the middle school high jump debacle didn't help. Then there was high school. The boys she knew in high school, well, they just seemed out of touch with the realities of life.

And she was afraid of being used and abused. There was this poor girl who got invited to the prom only to find her date abandon her after one dance. He only asked her so he wouldn't show up alone. Josy almost made a vow of celibacy, especially after the only date she went on in high school did not turn out so great. Her mom asked how it went and Josy said, "He's a jerk!" And that is all she would say about him.

She never felt like she fit in at high school She had few friends and was the only girl to take the BOCES Automotive class. Now, her classmates at BOCES were accepting of her and teased her like they did each other, but the kids at school were merciless. They called her "Grease Girl" and "Wrench Witch."

One time they plastered her locker with all kinds of nasty stuff. It was humiliating. She faked sickness for two days just to stay away.

That experience made her even more shy about attending any dances or parties. Her and her BOCES friends would work on small engines while others were off to who knows where. But when the county fair came around and her BOCES Auto class showed off the '67 Camero they restored...yeah...no name calling then...only 'oohs' and 'aahs.'

After graduation, many of her auto class mates got jobs in garages or car dealerships. But Josy stayed at the diner. She really didn't like the grease end of the wrench...she wanted to know about it, so she could be a better designer. At least that is what she told herself. It was fear that kept her away...she was afraid of not being taken seriously as a woman mechanic. It was bad enough to put up with the 'dirty old men' at the diner...not to mention the young ones too. If it wasn't for Mrs. Humphries who ran the diner with a firm hand, she might not feel safe there.

'Mama H.' as Josy called her, was like a second mother. And Mrs. Humphries called Josephine, 'Josy D.' She treated her like she was her own and always gave Josy good advice.

"You want to be a good waitress and get good tips? Then treat each customer as if they were your Gramma or Gramps. You do that and you'll make as much money as you want," she would say. "And those dirty old men? Just be stern, but always smile."

Josy did that, but she still had a fear of men, and for good reason.

It happened one evening at the gas station when a drunk pulled in. It was just before closing, around 9 pm. Mom and dad had left to get take-out and some groceries. This man, old Mr. Abernathy, had been at 'Happy Hour' for too long and was barely able to drive. He looked at Josy as he got out of his car and just kept staring. She did not know what to do. He had stared at her before, leering at her. He never got gas or anything, just would pull up, light a cigarette and stare at her before pulling away. It was a bit scary, but Josy's dad had always been right there…and she knew she was safe.

But this time, she was 14 and all alone with him. She tried to deflect her fear and his eyes by asking if he needed gas or oil. He said nothing and just kept staring at her. It seemed like forever before she said, "Okay, if there is nothing else, I'm closing now." She turned and hurriedly walked to the door closing it behind her as she turned the lock. Then she ran to the garage to close the overhead doors. As she pushed both down buttons, the old drunk began moving toward the doors. He was not fast, and didn't make it before the doors were almost down to the cement.

He began shouting and raving about what, she did not know. In the dim lights he looked like a monster. She ran back to the office phone and called the sheriff's office. She was just telling the desk sergeant about her predicament when Abernathy started banging on the doors and shouting. She knew she couldn't stay there.

Terrified, she ran from the office and into the apartment. But by then the drunken Abernathy had moved to the office door and started banging on the glass. It broke and he unlocked the door and went in. Josy quickly ran out the back door and was half way down the block when she looked back to see her mom and dad pull into the station with the sheriff right behind. Within minutes Mr. Abernathy was in handcuffs and she was in her mother's arms.

But the trauma of that night would haunt her in nightmares. And then there came the day Mr. Abernathy did a slow drive by. Her dad quickly came out with a long wrench and stared back. Mr. Abernathy drove away. Her dad turned, looked at her with a weary gaze, stared down at the ground, sighed and got back to work.

She did not know what to make of that. But, within minutes, her mom had gone to the sheriffs office. It was not a good thing to infuriate her mom. She was even-keeled, until she wasn't; and then you had better look out. After her mom's visit to the sheriff, Mr. Abernathy never came by the station again.

Sitting by her window remembering that experience, Josy realized she never got past that night, with those moments of terrible fear etched in her memory. Her dad had a scanner in the garage for accidents and she would listen to all the emergency, and police calls. That did not help her fears.

With a long sigh, Josy continued to stare out the window with the coffee cup halfway to her lips and thought, *So many bad things can happen...to innocent people. When you get old enough, that's when you find out how horrible human beings can be to each other.*

Her life experiences, the trauma at the station and other fears kept her at the diner, where she felt relatively safe. But Josy knew she couldn't stay there forever. And so, eventually, she took that civil service exam which led her to the D.M.V.

Lacey MacClean is never afraid. She looks at her fears and then walks all over them. What makes her dance is a deep down and absolute faith in her abilities and her God given talents. "Yes, that's it!" Josy said out loud, then laughing at herself for the outburst. But then, Josy thought, *Lacey is confident because she knows she is destined for something great. But what am I destined for?*

The coffee was cold now, and with another sigh...Josy took it to the microwave.

2

TIME OF DEATH: 10:37AM

It was 9:45 in the morning, Josy was busy at work 'pushing plates' when the call came in. She ran out to the Pinto praying it would start. It did, and she was off to the emergency room where her dad was being taken. He had just had a heart attack and was being given CPR. At least that's what her mom said was happening. She was driving as fast as she could with the old wagon and ran a few red lights in the process. It was early January and the wind was sweeping snow across the streets. She fishtailed into the parking lot and slid to a stop as she spied the ambulance. Her dad was being taken through the ER door on a stretcher with her mom in tow.

Her relationship with her mom and dad had been strange after the loss of the gas station. They seemed a bit aloof and never told her exactly why they had to close up the garage. She assumed it was the oil crisis, but never pressed for the reason because she also respected her parents greatly. They always protected and encouraged her. And after the Abernathy episode, they were even more protective.

It took a lot of convincing and a call from Mama H. to get them to let her begin working at the diner. "Mr. and Mrs. Daudry, don't you worry, I will look after your daughter as if my life depended on it. You hear me?"

Rushing into the ER she was suddenly met by a wall of fear. She stopped in her tracks. It was Abernathy! Really old and wrinkled now, in a wheelchair in the hallway just waiting. Josy was frozen in place. She felt like she couldn't move. All the memories of that night came rushing back. She wanted to turn and run. But then, her mom was suddenly there, standing before her blocking her view of him.

"Mom, mom! What's happening?" Josy asked as they rushed to the waiting area. Josy looked back. Abernathy was just staring...blankly.

As they sat down, all kinds of thoughts were crashing through Josy's mind. *What if dad dies? Oh...poor mom!* They had been married for nearly 35 years, and were, as they called themselves, 'soul mates.'

Another thought broke through. *Why is that &%@# Abernathy here?* It had been 16 years since she last saw him. *Why isn't he dead? God, why is this happening?*

Her mom saw Josy's face and tried to comfort her. "Your dad is strong, don't you worry. He will be fine. The Lord will take care of him."

The doctor came in. "Mrs. Daudry?"

Her mom got up, "Call me Sarah, Doctor. How is my Harry?"

It reminded Josy of the gas station. H & S Garage was the name on the big sign over the bay doors. But on the entry door her dad had another sign made, and it said, 'Sarah and Harry's Place.' *Dad always put moms' name first. He said, "She is the queen of my existence and I treat her as such in any way I can." Mom just smiled and said, "O Harry, don't be silly."*

Now, her best admirer was not so good. The doctors' news was scary. There would be an emergency quadruple by-pass and then they would see. One half of his heart was damaged. The prognosis was not great. If he survived the surgery, he would most likely be in the hospital for a long stay, and then the nursing care facility which was connected to the hospital. The doctor would look into putting him on the transplant list. There was no mention of when he could come home.

The hours in the waiting room passed by like a long line at a funeral home calling hours. You had to be there, wanted to be there, but were, at the same time, wanting to get out of there. Facing the realities of death is not easy. Especially for Josy, if it was her dads. Her mom was whispering prayers. Josy could make out the name of Jesus and the word please, repeated again and again.

Josy was not much of a prayer, but now she joined her mom. *It can't hurt. Right?* She thought to herself. And then she thought, *Would Lacey pray? Hell yeah, she would walk right in and say a prayer over dad, like those tent healers back in the day and heal him on the spot.* She chuckled to herself as she put her hand in her moms' and listened to her prayer.

A while later Mama H. showed up. It was like she was an angel from heaven. The winter storm had passed and the afternoon sunlight coming through the hospital window, just made her look etherial. "Mama H.!" Josy exclaimed as she gave her a big bear hug. "Josy D.!", was the reply.

"What are you doing here?", Josy asked.

"Well, I guess I'm here to see you. What's going on?"

After greeting her mom, and hearing about Harry, they all sat and prayed together. Then, this came over the loud speaker; "Mrs. Humphries, please come to the front desk." She excused herself and said, "I'll be back."

"Are you volunteering here?", Sarah asked.

"Yes, "After I retired, I figured I would give back to the town that has given me so much." She then disappeared around the wall as the doctor came in.

"Mrs. Daudry," the doctor said without expression.

"Please, call me Sarah."

"Yes, okay, Sarah. Well...the surgery was successful..."

Sarah just burst into tears and hugged the doctor before he could continue.

"Mrs. Daudry, Sarah, please listen. Yes, the surgery went well, but I must tell you that your husband's heart is barely able to function. Even if he recovers from this surgery, he will be debilitated. His heart will not be able to perform like it should. He should retire immediately and I will have our social worker help you with any disability forms. He will be in the hospital for at least three to four weeks and then most likely in the nursing care facility for an extended period."

Sarah just stood there, taking in the dire news. With Josy by her side, she turned to her and said, "Well, that's it, that is what we will be dealing with. We will get through it, Lord willing."

Josy was just glad her dad was still with them. But he was only 56 years old. Her mom was 7 years older than he. She had just retired a year before. Josy wondered how her mom would manage. Her dad was driving trucks over the road for a local company. Josy thought, *If forced to retire, what will happen to Dad's medical insurance? Without his insurance how can mom afford all the uncovered hospital expenses? How can we ever afford a heart transplant, even if he can get one?* Josy's mind was in a whirl. But her mom seemed calm.

"How are we going to manage this Mom? Financially?", Josy said this more as a statement of fear than a question to be answered. Her mom took her by the hands, looked her straight in the eyes and said, "I know you're worried, but it will be all right. We have been putting a little away each month and have some insurance for this sort of thing. We'll be okay."

Josy stayed with her mom at the hospital for 3 days until her dad was moved out of intensive care to a room. She only went home to shower and sleep. She took some personal time at her job so she could be there. Her mom would not leave her dad's side. The hospital put a roll-away bed in and let her use the shower in his room. It was a single-bed room, so it worked. Her dad never woke up until a day after the surgery. The doctors were concerned, but relieved when he finally awoke. He immediately reached for Sarah and Josy. They all hugged as best they could with all the tubes and wires all over his upper body. He couldn't speak. But he nodded as they both said how much they loved him. The next two days were spent just being there for him, getting him anything he needed. After the second day, he began to speak better and was a little cranky. "Pain, and being in bed are not setting well with my Harry", Sarah said to the nurse. "Let me see what the doctor can do.", she replied.

A week later Josy was giving her mom a break to go home and take care of things. She was sitting looking out the hospital window with a cup of coffee when her dad spoke up.

"I want one of those," he stated, firmly.

"One of what?".

"Coffee!" He raised his voice for emphasis.

"Oh, okay," and Josy got up in a flash. "I will get you a cup Dad." She headed straight out the door to the vending machines.

When she got back to the room, Mama H. was visiting with her dad. "Mama H.!", Josy exclaimed. "It's so good to see you. When did you get here?"

"Oh, I am just walking the halls and visiting folks like I do Tuesdays and Thursdays. I have been here a few times to see your dad and mom. I'm glad to see you too!"

They sat and talked about old times at the diner as her dad sipped his coffee. Josy talked about life at the D.M.V. She talked about still being in limbo after all these years, not knowing what she should do. She did not talk about her fantasy life of dreaming she was this 'Lacey MacClean', because she did not want to hurt her dad in any way... especially when it came to his ancestry (the family name) because she knew his ears were always tuned in to what she was saying. But this nagging longing in her heart was always there. So she skirted around that issue with other topics.

Mama H. listened and then said, "Well, I have to head on to the next room. But would you like me to say a prayer with you and your dad before I leave?" Now Josy had known Mama H. for years in the diner, but never heard her mention prayer or God. It was strange to think of this strong woman, who ran her business with a 'rod of iron', as talking about praying. And she did so with such a humble manner. It took Josy back a bit. Then she heard her dad say, "Yes, please do pray with us. And thank you. I can use all the prayers I can get." Again Josy was a bit shocked. Her dad was not the religious one in the family. That was her mom. Her dad never talked about anything but work, Josy's schooling or jobs. *I guess a heart attack can change a lot of things in a person,* she thought to herself.

Harry's boss, John Walker, came to see him on a Monday morning. Josy and her mom greeted him and thanked him for coming. "I am so sorry this has happened to Harry.", he said.

By then the social worker and the hospital billing clerk had talked with Sarah. It was not good news. Without insurance, even what they had saved would be eaten up in a hurry.

"How are you doing?", asked John.

"Well, we're okay...as well as can be expected. It is going to be a long road.", Sarah said.

Josy chimed in with, "And it won't be easy financially." She was going through the papers that the billing clerk had left.

"Josy!" Her mom exclaimed.

"So sorry, I...didn't mean to...it just hit me...the cost of all this."

"No need to apologize.", John said. "I understand. And listen, I have been thinking and talked it over with my wife and accountant. I am going to keep Harry on as an employee until his vacation time and sick time is up. And then I will continue to pay his health insurance as a retirement benefit until Medicare can kick in when he is 65. So that will cover most of this cost."

"You would do that?", Josy asked, tears welling up in her eyes.

Sarah said, "O John, that...that is so kind of you. Are you sure you can do that?"

"Yes, I can, and it is the least I can do for all the years Harry has given me. He is the best driver I have. He has earned every penny of what I can provide."

Hugs and handshakes all around; tears of thankfulness and sighs of relief enveloped the room. Harry looked at John with a knowing respect and shook his hand. He motioned for him to come closer and whispered something in his ear. John just gave him a look of assurance and left. Josy was talking in the corner with her mom, as John said, "Goodbye. I will be in touch."

After his departure, Josy said to her mom, "Even with the insurance from John's company...well...a transplant will be so costly...all the co-pays and meds. Mom, you said you had another insurance...what is it?" Sarah just hugged Josy and said quietly, our insurance is prayer, my dearest girl...prayer."

Josy stepped back and just looked at her mom. She turned with a sigh and rolled her eyes at that last comment. But then she turned back, leaned in, and said to her mom quietly, "Mom, Dad has been praying, well, at least he let Mama H. pray with him." "Yes, I know.", Sarah replied. "Small miracles...life is full of them."

Josy walked over to the window and thought about that. The morning was overcast, and the clouds were a light silver gray. But the sun was breaking through and the clouds were becoming a bright yellow white. Josy thought of how her mom certainly knew about miracles after she beat cancer...the tiredness, weakness and hair loss... and still, mostly, she just pushed on with such a positive attitude. It was a miracle she could be so gracious through it all. But what were some miracles in Josy's life? At that moment Josy could not think of any...another sigh. She said, "I'm going to get a coffee, do either of you want any?"

Just then her dad's face went ashen and his monitors started making all kinds of noises; she ran out and yelled for a nurse. Within seconds the room was full of nurses. She and her mom were asked to leave as a 'code blue' was sounding and a team was rushing in with a crash cart. A flurry of terms and orders were flying out of the doctor's mouth with the nurses responding in kind. She and her mom just stood outside the door hugging. There was so much noise coming from the room for what seemed like forever and then, a dead silence. After a moment they pushed back in the room. They could see the dejected faces and heard the doctor as she said with a steeled voice, "Time of death, 10:37am." She turned to Sarah and Josy and said she was so very sorry. She hovered for a moment holding Sarah's hand as the nurses began packing up the cart. Then, what seemed just as quickly as they all came, the team was gone and Sarah and Josy were left at her dad's side in shock.

They knew this could be a probable outcome, but still, it was so sudden they were beside themselves in silent grief. They just stood there staring at him in disbelief. Her mom began shaking, Josy went around the bed and hugged her from behind. Her mom started wailing, the disbelief gave way to realization, and it was heart wrenching. Through the sobs, her mom said, "I always thought I would leave him first. I figured my cancer would return someday and take me. This was not the way it's supposed to be. O, my Harry, my love." Josy could barely contain herself. She wanted to keep it together for her mom, but began convulsively sobbing as well. They both hugged her dad as best they could, tubes, electrodes and all. They cried and cried together.

They didn't notice the nurse standing in the room silently with his head bowed. He finally came around where they could see him. He gently said that he could get Harry cleaned up a bit without all the tubes and things so they could be with him easier, and that they could stay there as long as they needed to. They were appreciative and let him begin his work as they sat by the window shaking their heads and holding hands. The charge nurse came in and said that if they wanted, there was a Chaplain on call for these situations, and they could have a visit if so desired. Sarah nodded and Josy said, "Please do. Thank you." A few minutes later the Chaplain came in. It was Mama H.

3

MAMA H.

It had been a few weeks since the funeral, where long lines snaked their way through the calling hours and then the service following. As Josy was in her mom's guest room, napping...sort of...mostly remembering how she and her mom greeted all the folks, and the thankfulness they felt for the outpouring of heartfelt wishes...it all suddenly overwhelmed her. She had to get to a window.

It was always her favorite place, especially with a cup of coffee...or in the evening with chamomile tea. Her mom's house had a beautiful window seat and that is where she headed. Many a visit to her mom and dad's she would take naps there. The window seat was lined with built in book shelves full of novels of all kinds, and especially her favorite Celtic historical novels.

As she was making herself a cup, she thought, *I never knew Dad and Mom had that many friends and acquaintances. It seemed like the whole village was there.* The photos were admired by all, and there were so many cards. The funeral home even put together a VHS tape of the pictures with music. It had been playing in the background. Now it sat on the coffee table with all the funeral papers and photos in a box they brought home. *I guess we will have to get Mom a VCR now*, Josy thought.

The food from all the friends and family that had been dropped at Sarah's home was now going to waste. The nieces and their kids had stayed the weekend along with Sarah's brother and his wife. But now they were gone and Josy and her mom just picked at the food. Without the family it just seemed like a chore to eat. Josy had used up her personal time and vacation time. She had to get back to work soon.

Sarah said to her, "I'll be okay. You have to get back to your home and work. Don't worry about me." Josy just had a blank look on her face as she sat across from her mom on the upholstered window seat.

She finally said with a half cry, "Mom, I just don't know what to do, I am dreading going back to work. Everyone knows how much I loved Dad, and I am not looking forward to the 'so sorry' comments and the looks of pity. And worse than that are those who will avoid me all together."

Sarah replied, "O honey, you don't know that will happen."

"O yes I do Mom, 'cause that is how I reacted to Mama H. when she lost her son. I just couldn't deal with it. I didn't know what to say. I wanted to help but I couldn't. It was horrible, I feel like I failed her."

"Now darling, I know for a fact Eleanor doesn't feel like you have ever failed her. She is your 'Mama H.' and you are her 'Josy D.' and nothing could change that." "I know that", Josy replied. "But I still feel bad. I am almost 33, and I still feel like I'm a teenager! Why am I like this?" Her mom did not have an answer. Josy, seeing there were no words of wisdom coming, sighed, sipped her tea and blankly stared out at the snowy trees.

It was dark, and the Christmas lights were buried under the snow ladened branches. It was February now, but there were still boxes with her dad's presents in them under the tree which normally would have been all stored away by now. Neither of them had the heart to take it down.

Harry was all about Christmas decorations. The whole house was his Christmas playground. When he and Josy would go shopping for presents for her mom, Sarah would say, "Don't let your dad go anywhere near the decorations! We have more than enough." But there was always some little, or big decoration, that he thought his Sarah 'must' have. But really, it was for him. Decorating the house gave him a pleasure he did not get anywhere else. So Josy and her mom would just, sigh together and let it go with a knowing smile.

Now, those memories were all they had and it was painful when it would hit them. Tears would well up, and sometimes sobs were just unavoidable. Mama H. had told them in the hospital the day Harry died that this was coming, and it would be normal. "Grief has no timetable" She said.

Mama H., as Chaplain came that awful morning in January and sat with Sarah and Josy for a long while in the hospital room. She had brought in a tray with drinks and snacks that the hospital supplied. Not much of it was touched until Sarah finally spoke, "Thank you for being here with us, Eleanor.", she said as she opened an apple juice.

Mama H responded, "There is no other place for me right now."

After they all had a bite, she even did some kind of a service over Harry's body. Josy didn't remember much of it except the 23rd Psalm and the Lord's Prayer, but it seemed to give her some comfort. She did not understand that. Sure, her mom would want that and appreciate it, but Josy?

I never have been like Mom in the way of faith, she thought. *Dad and I never bought into that...well at least that is what I thought.* She remembered her dad praying that last week of his life. Not only when Mama H. was there, but also he and her mom prayed together. Josy sat and watched them, the two love birds she always admired. *I didn't tell them enough how I loved them when they were together*, she thought.

Now, all that Mama H. did and said, and didn't say, came to Josy's mind. She got up from the window seat and found her mom in the kitchen.

"What am I going to do with all this food?" Sarah said, as she held on to the counter with both hands. Josy just gave her a big hug and said, "I love you Mom. It will be all right."

Her mom backed out of the embrace and shook her head. "I...am... so....I just don't understand...why?" She broke down crying.

Josy never saw her mom like this. It shook her to the core. Her mom was always stronger than she and her dad. Now she was this stricken widow banging her hands on the counter and sobbing. Josy had no idea what to do, so she called Mama H.

It took a while for Mama H. to arrive. By then Sarah had calmed down somewhat and Josy decided to get rid of the oldest food so that at least her mom wouldn't have to deal with it. She was washing containers when the doorbell rang.

"That will be Mama H.", Josy called out to her mom.

Sarah opened the door. "Welcome Eleanor", she said. "Come in, although it wasn't necessary for you to come over this late."

Josy left the kitchen sink and joined them at the table. Mama H. just started talking about old times and memories. Pretty soon they were laughing and crying. Coffee, tea and cookies seemed to help the mood.

Sarah excused herself. When she went to the bathroom, Josy looked at Mama H. and said, "I am a little worried about Mom. She is not herself, and I understand that, but she is even questioning God. That is not like her."

Mama H. replied, "My dear, it is okay to question everything including God. It certainly doesn't bother the Spirit, to be questioned. And in this situation, believe me, I know, it is definitely normal."

Josy, knew that was a reference to losing her son to an aneurism at age 21. Those were dark days at the diner, uncomfortable days. Josy spoke softly, "Can I ask how you got through your loss of David?"

Mama H. just stared at her cup of tea and took a long deep breath. "Some wise man told me this, 'All you can do is take one step forward at a time, every moment of every day. Sometimes the memories will throw you down like a wet rag, other times they will lift you up like a feather on the breeze.' You see, Josy, grief is a deep expression of the great love you have for someone who has died. It is normal, and the grieving process is the only way to get through the trauma of it all. It is not easy, but necessary."

Josy suddenly burst out with it... "O Mama H., I am so sorry for not being there for you during that time!"

"O honey, it's okay, you were just a child."

"I was 22.", Josy said quietly.

"Oh, It's hard enough for mature adults to deal with death and grief. You were a young 22, so don't be too hard on yourself."

"I just don't know how to help Mom", Josy said with a sigh. "Lacey would know what to do." It just slipped out. Mama H. eyed Josy with a questioning look.

Just then Sarah came back and Josy hoped that her comment would just fade away. When it was getting late, prayers were said, and Josy saw Mama H. to the door. "I would like to have a lunch with you, say next week?"

Before the door closed Eleanor turned back and said, "Yes, I would like that Josy. I could meet you at the diner, say Friday at noon?"

"Done.", said Josy. "Goodnight."

Coming back to Humphries Diner was nostalgic. The new owners wisely kept the name. They kept the great cook, Frank, and kept up the friendly service too. Josy and Mama H sat at the counter just looking around with memories flowing in their minds eye. The waitress said she would be right with them, but they said they were waiting for a booth. "There should be one soon.", said the waitress.

The cook, Frank, could see them through the warming shelf and came around to say hello. "Aah Mrs. Humphries, it's so good to see you! And you too Josy! How's it going?"

"We are well, Frank. And you?", Mama H. replied.

"Oh, I'm cook'n." He said with a laugh, as he went back to the grill.

"You never get tired of that one, Frankie," Josy said.

"No…I don't," he chuckled.

The corner booth opened up and they moved over so they could talk. After ordering Mama H. asked, "So, Josy D., why are we here? Is this just a visit or do you have something you want to talk about?"

"Well, I have a few questions," Josy said. "How did you come to be a Chaplain? I thought you were just a volunteer…an older like…um…a candy striper. And about that…you're religious now? Were you always? I have to say, I never thought of you that way. I mean…I am not putting you down for it…I just did not expect you to be 'that' person in the hospital. And let me add, you were the best! Mom and I would not have got through that day without you."

"Okay, okay," Mama H. pushed in. "That's enough questions."

"O, I'm sorry Mama H., it's just that I have had time to think these last few weeks…and." Josy stopped talking as their drinks came.

"It's okay," Mama H. softly said. "Well, let me see…where to begin."

She took a deep breath. "After David died, I was sitting there in the ER with no one. I was fumbling around my purse trying to find David's dad's phone number to call him and let him know about the tragedy when a person was standing beside me. It was the Chaplain. He was kind hearted and just sat with me. He listened to me intently as I raged at life, God, who or whatever that was, and my ex-husband for leaving me alone to raise this boy who now lay lifeless on a gurney. There was a kindness to him I had not experienced in many men, especially at the diner.

"By the time midnight had rolled around he had helped me call David's dad, get food and coffee, met with me and the charge nurse to set up which funeral home would come for David's body and I don't remember what else. I was so thankful, that I got his card. I would call him from time to time when I was feeling low and he would say a prayer for me. And then, he started showing up to the diner to see how I was. One day I asked him why he did what he did. I knew it couldn't be easy facing folks who lost loved ones this way on a weekly or daily basis. I asked if he ever felt burned out. He said that yes, it could be draining and one has to take care of themselves, but that overall it is a need that he was thankful that he could help meet.

"One day, about a year later, he was in the diner and it was slow so I sat down with him. He said, 'Eleanor, you know, I have watched you here at the diner this last year and I must tell you, you have a gift.'

'What...me?' I said in disbelief.

'Yes, you,' He answered. 'I have seen you with people here and I'm telling you, you should think about doing what I do.'

I just shook my head and said, 'Not me, I could never do what you do.'

He replied, 'You're already doing it. Every time I come here, I see you with folks; comforting them, laughing with them, but most importantly, listening to them. One of the greatest lines in any book or movie is this: "I see you." Which means to really hear a person, to truly behold them, to value them, to listen...truly listen to them.

'People talk with each other all the time, but I have observed in myself and others that they don't really listen. When one is talking... the other is really just thinking of what they want to say next. I catch myself doing this sometimes. But to really listen, is to truly see someone, let what they are saying enter your mind and heart. To listen is one of the greatest gifts we can give each other. When I don't listen that way, what I am doing is making a snap judgement that what they are saying is, well, not that important; which is the opposite of listening and it can be so destructive, because when a person is not listened too, they shrink away from you and possibly life itself.

'Now I have watched you, Eleanor, and I can say with confidence that you don't judge anyone, you just listen and empathize. You have the personality, the patience and the heart to do this. And it is so needed. I am asking you to think about it and pray.'

"So I did. You see Josy, after David died, sometimes in the evening I would drive aimlessly around the town. One time I saw this church. The name of it...'St. David's Episcopal Church.' It seemed like a sign. So I began going and just sitting. I didn't say much, but just let my soul cry silently. I was like a little child, rocking back and forth. I did this for many months, I don't know how long.

"The priest came over to me one day and said, 'I know you Mrs. Humphries, I have seen your diner's ads in the paper and saw the news about your son. If there is anything I can do for you, please let me know.'

"So, to make a long story short, eventually, he directed me to a group of other parents who had lost children. It was in that group of loving people that I began to see God. It wasn't a flash of lightning but a gradual realization of faith.

"So when the Chaplain laid out the challenge to me that day at the diner, I did pray about it and asked my pastor and the group about it. The encouragement was overwhelming. I never saw myself as being in a 'ministry' but they all said that I already was, at the diner, and that maybe it was God calling me to a different place.

"So I prayed, 'Lord if this is what you want...then sell my diner to someone I can trust to treat the people the way I always have.' Two years later it all came together and I finished my schooling...and here I am. Now, does that answer your questions Josy?"   "I suppose so.", Josy answered. "I agree you have a gift for listening and giving good advice."

"Well, now I have a question for you Josy; who is Lacey?"

4

THE LOGBOOK

*J*osy looked out the diner window watching the snow drifting along the street. It formed lines that were like waves. It reminded her of her life...just being pushed along by the wind...no real direction.

"Josy" Mama H. interrupted her thoughts in an easy tone. "Are you going to answer me? Who is Lacey?"

"Ahh...ummm...well..." Josy was trying to think of ways to tell her trusted friend of how she was like a pre-teen with these fantastical thoughts of Lacey MacClean.

"Okay, if you don't want to tell me that is fine. It's just that you said her name as if she was a friend you could count on...you said, 'Lacey would know what to do,' and I had never heard you speak of her ever before. Is she someone from the D.M.V.?"

Josy became a little annoyed, "You really do listen...don't you?"

"That is what I do.", she replied, with a smile.

Josy took a deep breath…"Ok…Lacey MacClean…that's her full name and…she is not…well…she is not real. There! I said it. She is my… alter ego I guess. I fantasize about being her. She has it all together and is an F1, that is a Formula One driver. Beautiful deep red hair…you know…everything I'm not."

Mama H. just sat there, nodded her head as she listened and then she said, "Okay, so…I would like to get to know this Lacey MacClean. Would you mind introducing her to me? Tell me all about her and what it is that you admire about her."

Josy just stared at her…that was not the reaction she expected.

Just then Frank came out from the kitchen "Hey Josy, I just got a call from your mom. She needs you to come to her house as soon as you're done with your lunch."

"Is something wrong?"

"I don't think so…she didn't sound upset, but she does want you to come as soon as you can."

Josy and Mama H. quickly said their goodbyes. Josy left cash for the check and headed out the door. As they parted in the parking lot, Mama H. said, "Josy, if you ever want to tell me about Lacey…I meant what I said."

Josy nodded and got into the Pinto, thought a moment about what she would say to Mama H., and then got frustrated with the Pinto, which, of course, would not start.

Mama H. had just pulled away, so Josy was left there. She went back in and told Frank she needed a jump.

"In this cold wind, the battery is not working the best.", she said.

"No problem, the lunch rush is over, I will be right out."

Josy was swearing at the old car as she headed down the street, and wondering how she managed to let her secret slip out to Mama H. *I need my coffee and my window,* she thought to herself as she pulled in the driveway to her mom's place; a little house that her mom and dad bought after he was working at the trucking firm for a while. Her mom also got a job at the bank where she managed all the tellers until she retired.

The house was a bungalow and the best feature was the window seat that Josy had claimed as her own. It was her safe place, to wonder, dream, read and fantasize. As she walked in the door, and now that her secret was exposed, the window didn't seem as inviting as usual. Something had changed.

Sarah greeted Josy and directed her to the kitchen table where John Walker was sitting with a black book. Greetings were exchanged and cups of coffee were poured.

"John, do you want a sandwich?" Sarah asked.

"No thanks. I just ate lunch." He said

"So what is going on?" Josy asked with a little trepidation.

John looked at Sarah and she nodded.

John began...."Well, Josy, you see this ledger, it was your dad's logbook for his travels last year. The logbook keeps track of mileage, loads, returns...that sort of thing. But there is something else. This last year, he also started writing notes…kinda like a diary of sorts. If they were just in the back of the book, I would have taken out those pages and given them to you. But he intermingled them with the business entries. So I can't separate them. I need you and Sarah to read them, and if you want, you can make a copy of those pages...but then I need the ledger back."

Josy looked a little bewildered and then said, "I would have never thought my dad would keep a diary." She looked at her mom who just dodged her eye contact and stared down at the table.

"Mom, did you know about this?", she asked.

"No, I did not. But, I can imagine some of the things that Harry wrote in there and I have to warn you Josy, it may not be easy to read or accept."

Josy didn't respond to that statement. She shook her head and then looked at John. "Did you read it?"

"Well, I did see some things, but tried to skip over them. And your dad did tell me some things in confidence, one father to another. But, this is for you and your mom. I have done what Harry asked me to do that day in the hospital, and now I will leave you both. But if you need to talk or have questions, just give me a call. And when you are done with it, please let me know and I will come back to get it."

The logbook sat on the coffee table for a while. Neither Sarah nor Josy were ready to get into it. It was early March; Josy had gone back to work but came over to her mom's for dinners most nights. They would look at it, sitting there, like a bomb with countdown going faster and faster. Sarah finally said on Josy's birthday evening, "It's time Josy, we need to read the logbook."

"You know what is in there don't you Mom."

"Well, my dear, I have not read it, but I know the things that made your dad happy and the things that haunted your dad. So I think I do know some things that will be there. "But we will read it together and whatever is there we will deal with it... good or bad, happy or sad."

"But today? It's my birthday Mom."

"Well, all right, let's wait 'til next week."

Three weeks went by and finally Sarah brought the book to the dinner table and with a firm tone said, "After we eat, we will read this. Okay?"

"Okay, Mom, I think I am ready.", Josy replied.

The book was a little larger than letter size and the cover was well worn. The sheets were three hole punched and they were held in by metal clasps that went through and folded in the back. The sheets looked like there was a slide rule across them near the top and they had a continuous line going over and down and back up, over some more and up and down.

Upon a closer look, it was an hours chart. The line coincided with hours that were delineated on the top and bottom of the chart. The line indicated when her dad was driving, sleeping or was taking time off to eat or shower. Under the hours chart there was a white space with names of cities with diagonal lines drawn down from the hour he arrived. And under that was his name, the total miles, and other info. But over to the far right was a space...after the last city he came to, and that is where he kept his diary entries. There really wasn't much room, so the entries were short.

Just like my dad, Josy thought, *He was never a talker.*

Harry had driven for Walker Trucking for 14 years and so there was a lot of miles on the road. "What would have caused your dad to start a diary, and only this last year?" Sarah wondered out loud as they made their way to the window seat.

Josy said, "Maybe he knew...well anyway...let's read them."

They sat down and started reading with January of 1992. Not every day had a 'diary' entry but there were some weeks where he wrote 3 or 4 days, and some other weeks only one day. They started reading from the beginning. January 6 showed her dad leaving with a load for Georgia with stops in West Virginia and North Carolina. After he arrived in Atlanta, he made a note that he had to remember to stop at Bingham's restaurant on the way back up Route 81 to get some of their cream puffs for Sarah. 'My honey loves her sugar.' He noted.

Many of the entries were like that. It seemed he was using the log book as a memory bank. On February 14 he was headed back from Cleveland and just got into the Buffalo hub. He noted that he could not wait to get home to give Sarah and Josy the Valentines gifts he picked up in Kalamazoo.

The entry for March 17 was special for Josy. He noted that since he would not be home for her St. Patty's Day birthday celebration, he would have to drink some green beer without her, but would call from the rest stop. And when he got home on Friday, he would take them out for a good dinner wherever they wanted. He noted that he had to stop and pick up the gift he had ordered the week before at the Indianapolis Speedway store. 'She'll love these tickets for next year's 500.', he wrote.

Reading that entry made them both burst into tears. That Memorial Day weekend the three of them had traveled to the Indy 500 and had a great time. They had made quite a few trips there over the years, but now the realization that last year's was Harry's final trip to Indy made them cry. They took a break from reading and went to the kitchen to eat a snack.

Afterward, Josy went back to the window and kept looking at the entries. She turned the pages and came to August 19th. It was a Wednesday and her dad had pulled into a truck stop near Denver for the night. The entry was not the usual...full of loving things for and about her and her mom. This was dire. It read, "Aug. 19...the worst day of my life! How I wish I could go back in time and just check that brake line again. Damn that day. O that beautiful little Laney...poor George and Ellie...poor Sarah and Josy. O Lord, have mercy."

"Mom!" Shouted Josy. She ran to the kitchen where Sarah was just cleaning up and said, "What is this?" Her mom asked what she meant. "Read it Mom. Just read it.", Josy demanded.

Sarah read and then sat down at the table. "O my dear child...my dear, dear child."

Josy sat down next to her and asked, "What is it Mom? Who is Laney…George and Ellie?"

Sarah just stared at the table. She shook her head, got up and went back to the window seat. They both sat down and looked out at the spring evening. It had rained that day and the trees were still dripping. A tear came to Sarah's eyes as she turned to tell Josy what it all meant.

She started, "It was…the day from hell. August 19,1959…I was pregnant for you, just 2 months along when suddenly I started bleeding. Your dad was working on…(she paused)…then said tentatively… George's…(another pause)…well it was Mr. Abernathy's car."

Josy closed her eyes, shook her head and exclaimed, "What? Mr. Abernathy? I don't understand."

So many emotions suddenly came rushing into Josy's mind. It was only a couple of months ago she saw him in the ER. It had been a long time since the incident at the garage but it was always with Josy. Back then there was not much talk about trauma or PTSD as they now called it. Nowadays, with the war in Kuwait over, it was talked about, but in the 70's not so much. You just had to deal with these things on your own. Josy thought about getting counseling as she grew older, but never did and her parents never talked about it. That was not what their generation did. Everything got swept under the rug, as it were.

Sarah put her hands on Josy's shoulder and continued. "Honey, I am so sorry to have to tell you all this…I probably should have sooner, but your dad…well anyway, listen and try not to get too upset. As I said, I was bleeding and your dad had to get me to the hospital right away. He was under Mr. Abernathy's car fixing the brakes and quickly finished connecting them. He was wiping his hands on the rag as we got into the car and rushed off to the ER. Now, I was fine after a few days rest. And the pregnancy went fine after that. But we were so scared that I was going to lose you. I have told you about me having a miscarriage before. We were so scared.

"But anyway, and here is where it gets horrible." Sarah took a deep breath and continued. "At the ER, they examined me and admitted me. That all took a long time, so after it was clear I was not going to lose you, your dad called Mr. Abernathy to tell him the car was done and that the big doors were open. If he needed the car, he could take it, the keys were in it. And they could settle up when he got back, and he asked him to close the doors.

"So Mr. Abernathy, George, did just that. He got the car and then went home to his daughter Laney and her mom, Ellie. A week later they all took the car to go somewhere, I don't remember, but...there was an accident. You see the brake line came loose...Harry, in the rush to get me to the hospital, didn't tighten it all the way. So over the next few days it loosened up until if finally started leaking fluid. George never noticed it in his gravel driveway.

"Now your dad always double checked things like that, but not that day...not in that moment. His mind was on me and my unborn baby... you. So, little Laney, that's what they called her, just 6 years old, was killed that day."

Josy just closed her eyes, bent over with her hands to her face and cried out... "O my God! No!"

Sarah said, "I am so sorry. We were so sorry. George and Ellie were devastated. Your dad was beside himself when he realized it was his mistake. That was a hard time, but Ellie was able to forgive your dad's error. She understood he was scared for me and my baby. She was okay, but not George. He vowed to 'make you pay' he would say.

"After Ellie died in '71 he began drinking heavily. And, as you know, he looked at you with longing eyes... I think maybe, he saw in you, his daughter Laney. And he was....umm... I don't know if jealous is the right term, but when he got drunk he would sit at the bar and rant about our family. Your dad heard him one time and tried to talk to him, but when he was drunk like that, it was of no use."

Josy was bent over...her face in her knees this whole time. It was too much. Her life was spared but another precious life was taken. Then it all made sense. That night when Mr. Abernathy was at the garage in his drunken state, this was the reason.

"What was he going to do that night Mom?"

"You mean that night he was arrested? Well, we don't know for sure. The sheriff thought he might want to kidnap you or harm you...he was so drunk we couldn't get a straight answer. The next day, the sheriff reported that George was so sorry and certainly never meant to cause you any harm. Your dad always felt so bad that he didn't want to cause George any more pain. He would have been willing to let it all go, but it was 'breaking and entering' so the sheriff had to arrest him.

"When he did that drive by a while later, I had had enough. I took the sheriff with me and we confronted George. He was just crying. The sheriff said he needed to get help, which he promised to do. And I assume he did because he never came around again...but then..."

Josy interrupted, "I need to go, Mom...I just need to go."

"But dear ", Sarah replied, "we should talk the rest of this through together."

Josy, looking out the window said, "The rest?...Aah...no... I need to go."

She gathered her purse and coat and left with her mom standing in the doorway with the logbook in her hand.

5

THE WINDOW SEAT

Josy got in the Pinto wagon and drove past her apartment house. She wasn't ready to go home. She went by the old garage and stopped out front. It was empty now. There hadn't been a business there for a while. She thought about going to a bar and getting drunk...but she never did the bar scene. Besides when she thought of getting drunk, all she could think about was Mr. Abernathy. She pulled away and drove past the diner. She thought about calling Mama H., but it was late. She drove by St. David's and thought about going in. She was not ready for that, even if it worked for Mama H. She sighed...and then headed north.

She drove all the way to Lake Ontario and sat there in a restaurant parking lot all night...thinking and crying. Not knowing what to make of it all. Her thoughts were racing...*Why didn't Dad ever tell me? Why did Mom keep the secret? So what if that is the way it was done back then. I would have understood, even if I was only 14. It was wrong to keep it from me all these years. It was selfish of Mom and Dad...they just didn't want to face it with me. They were cowards.*

She turned on the radio and just let the tunes ease her mind. *Bridge Over Troubled Water* came on, and she felt as if Simon and Garfunkel were singing it just for her. She grabbed a sleeping bag from the back and snuggled in the foggy spring night. She was able to drift off for a bit, but sleep was fitful most of that night. Finally, the sun came over the horizon. The light crept into her eyes and she awoke to the morning. The clouds were gone and there were April tulips in the sculpted medians of the parking lot. She rolled down her window and took in the scents of spring. As she did, she realized she was hungry and needed a good hot cup of coffee, plus...the bathroom. She let the sleeping bag fall off grudgingly and hurried into the restaurant.

As Josy was eating, it suddenly hit her. It was a work day, and she needed to get to the D.M.V. by 9am! She quickly stuffed the rest of her breakfast down and ran out to the car. It was 7:30 and she had to hightail it south if she was going to be on time. No time to go home and shower. *Yesterday's clothes will have to do,* she thought.

But then, of course, the Pinto would not start. She had fallen asleep with the radio on. The battery was dead. She called the car a few choice names. No way would she get to work on time now. She went back in to the restaurant to use the pay phone. Calling work sheepishly, she was hoping her supervisor would be there early, as she usually was, and be understanding. The phone rang and rang until the answering machine picked up, began its long message, and then she realized...it was Saturday. Relief was a welcome feeling. She took a deep sigh, sat down at her table, which was now being cleared. She asked for another cup of coffee.

"I know I just ate, but I need more," she said to the young man who had waited on her.

"No problem," he said. "And would you like one of our famous cinnamon buns? I can warm it up for you."

Josy nodded yes, answering, "Why not."

The restaurant had a huge window overlooking the lake and, as the sun rose higher in the sky, the white caps were glistening. *Thank goodness for this view,* she thought. *Without windows in my life what would I do?* In her mind she could hear what her Grandma used to say: *"God paints the most beautiful pictures in the sky...just there for someone to notice, if they feel so inclined."* A thought occurred to Josy, *Was this painting in the sky just for me?*

A feeling of warm thanksgiving came over her. She certainly needed that sky painting after last night's darkness. She thought about her judgements of her mom and dad. And then she remembered what Mama H. said about listening being a gift. She suddenly knew she had to get back to her mom.

She asked about a jump from the waiter and he said there was a station just around the corner. He would give them a ring. Josy thanked him and anxiously waited for them to come. Standing by the Pinto, looking at the skyline, she took a long look at her life as the mechanic began his work. She felt a new sense of who she was and why she was. It was the hidden things that kept her chained to that day back in '74. Just like Aug 19, 1959 kept her dad and mom and Mr. Abernathy in chains. Chains of fear and loss, chains of anger. *How could they all break free?* She wondered.

"Miss" The mechanic woke Josy out of her thoughts.

"Let's give it a try, shall we?" Josy said yes, got in the car, and turned the key.

"It's a good thing it's Saturday," she said as she got out of the car with cash in hand to pay the man. Yesterday was payday, otherwise I'd be paying you by changing some oil."

He looked at her funny.

"Oh, I used to work for my mom and dad at their garage," she said. And then a sudden wave of memories of her dad came over her. How he used to tease her and her mom with dirty rags and unwashed hands. One time he had a big glob of grease on his face and insisted on giving her mom a big fat kiss. She ran away from him. "You better not! You're cruising buddy, you're cruising!" Josy let out a laugh and then almost burst into tears. She quickly composed herself and said, "Thank you."

But then, the mechanic said, "It's you! Josy, it's you! I thought I recognized you. It's been a while. Remember me from auto class? It's Greg, Greg Watkins."

"O my goodness! Greg! Of course I remember," she answered. "It's been a long time. How are you?"

"I'm good. Are you okay? You seem a little upset."

"Well, this old car..." She stopped herself, "It's not the car...well it is...but really...it's my dad. He died just a few months ago and..."

"I understand," Greg broke in. I lost my sister 5 years ago and it still hits me sometimes."

They chatted for a few minutes and then parted with talk of having a coffee sometime as he handed her his card and she gave him her phone number.

Josy thought to herself, *Wow, I never expected to see Greg again.*

Greg waved to Josy as she drove away. She didn't see him. She was focused on getting home and she hoped her mom wasn't too upset. She wanted to listen to her mom's side of things. How did she feel that day. And how did she cope? *I want to start listening and not judging so quickly.* She thought, *I have wasted so much time judging... myself mostly... too much time.*

Josy pulled into her mom's driveway to find her mom outside tending to her flower garden. She just eyed her mom with admiration. All her negative thoughts the night before were washed away in love and empathy. She just wanted to let her know she understood and wanted to help her through this time. Josy got out of the car as her mom got up and they met by the Rose of Sharon bush with a big hug.

"I'm so sorry," Sarah said.

"I'm sorry too, Mom."

There was a silence as they let go of their hug. Then Josy said, "So... Mom, we're both sorry...let's move out of sorryville to helperville. I'll help you and you help me. Okay?"

"Deal," her mom replied. "Now, speaking of help...you can help me get this soil turned before we have some coffee."

"Sure, but I'm kinda coffee-d out, I have had a lot this morning."

"Where were you?" Sarah asked.

"It's a long story. I will tell you over a cup of tea and a tall glass of water later."

Sitting at the window seat again felt wonderful as the late morning sun poured through. Sarah brought the hot drinks and some shortbread. As she sat down, Josy said, "This window...I just love it. I know you know that Mom. But I have to say it is just so warm and inviting this morning."

"Why is that? What is the attraction for you my dear?"

"Well," Josy thought a minute. "Besides the coffee or tea...which on a cold day makes you feel so cozy...it's all the books, the cushion and pillows...and then, it's nature...it's always just outside my window. You know it's all the beauty out there, especially the sky...the blue, the incredible blue...and the clouds, the shapes and colors...rainbows... the mid-day sun and at night the sunsets and the moon and stars...just beautiful. And it all seems to make me feel beauty inside myself."

Sarah replied, "Well, creation is God's gift to us. Humans are the only beings on this planet who can appreciate it...if we can take the time to see it...feel it...listen to it and care for it."

Josy just took in that statement and then replied, "You know Mom, I am not like you about God. But I do believe in what you just said about nature and learning to listen. Nature or creation as you call it, has a lot to say to me sometimes. And I do want to pay more attention. In fact the sunrise over the lake this morning really kinda saved me."

"The lake?" Sarah asked, "You were all the way up there?"

"Well, yes Mom, I just had to get away last night. It was just a lot to take in. But a night in my old wagon was just what I needed."

"All night in that car? Why didn't you get a motel room?"

"Well, I just was sitting there listening to the radio and fell asleep. And of course, in the morning, the car wouldn't start."

"O that old car...you need to buy a new one, Josy!" Sarah exclaimed. "Someday that car is going to get you in real trouble."

"O Mom, don't worry," Josy said. "And it was funny, I met an old high school buddy from auto class...he came to my rescue. And anyway the sunrise was so beautiful and I remembered what Grandma use to say about taking time to notice 'Gods painting in the sky'...you remember what she used to say...anyway it was a great morning."

Sarah took a deep breath and said, "I am so glad to hear you say that. It seems that maybe you have come to terms with some things I told you last night?"

"Come to terms?...I am not sure you could say that, but I am trying to understand it all...and I want to try to forgive...all of you for keeping it from me."

As they cleared the tea cups and shortbread plate to the kitchen, the door bell rang. Sarah said, "O that must be Eleanor. I invited her over for lunch today. I was hoping you would be here too."

"I'll get the door," Josy said. She was glad to see Mama H.

"Josy D.!" Mama H. said as she came through the door. "I'm so glad to see you. I heard that I drove off too quickly from the diner last month when you got that call from your mom. I am so sorry."

"No worries, it was fine, Frankie helped me out. Can I take your coat?"

Mama H. said, "Sure." They went to the kitchen table where Sarah was pulling cold cuts and fixings from the fridge. "It's not going to be fancy today; a little of this, a little of that and not much of anything." She said as she pulled chips out of the pantry.

They sat down and began to eat and talk. Sarah told Eleanor about the logbook and the rest of the tale. Mama H. listened and said nothing as she ate. There was a large archway between the kitchen and family room. From where Josy was sitting she could catch the window seat's view. Spring was setting in nicely as buds were opening on the trees and daffodils and snow drops were already starting to fade.

Sarah finished telling Eleanor the story and said, "Well, I suppose that was a lot to take in, and I'm sorry to tell it all to you, but I value your opinion and your help with ways we can deal with this."

Mama H. replied, "Well, as Jesus said, 'The truth will set you free.' And it can only help to talk about it all."

Josy turned to her mom, "Mom, I know you didn't finish last night before I took off. What did you not say?"

"Oh, yes, well, it's about the station. The reason we had to close… aah…maybe it's not important now."

"The truth is always important," Eleanor interjected.

"It's okay Mom, I can handle it now," said Josy.

"Okay," Sarah said. "Well, here it is...After Ellie died, George went about telling everyone he met about what happened, that is... when he was tipsy. As long as Ellie was alive he would not, and he never said a word when he was sober. Drunkenness made him angry. That's when he raged about Laney's death and your father's mistake that led to it. And the word travels fast in bars and people began not coming to our garage anymore. It just was not sustainable. We could not move the station...we just had to close it."

"But how did he know it was Dad's fault?" asked Josy. "Maybe he hit a rock or something that caused the line to leak."

"No, your Dad inspected the car after the wreck. He said it was clear that the connection came unscrewed. He told George and Ellie about his mistake…he was so heartbroken. I have never seen him cry like that. It was all so sad, just…so sad. And Ellie understood. She knew his mind was on me and my fears of a miscarriage. George was so grief stricken that he could not even talk. It was so hard those days. And as the years went by it was just a thing none of us talked about.

"After Ellie died, I think George felt so alone, and that's when he started to drink heavily. You know, when we finally had to close the gas station, let me see, it was...um...19 years after the accident; your dad and I both felt a relief to be out of there. It was just a part of our life we were ready to leave behind."

Josy asked, "Why didn't you leave earlier?"

Sarah took a long sigh, a bite of her sandwich, swallowed, and answered. "Well, we were still young and new parents, and had so much invested, that we really couldn't do anything but keep going. Then I got cancer, so that consumed all our extra time; and that next year you began working for us, that made us feel closer to you and then, well, time goes so fast...suddenly it was 1978...you were graduating and so it seemed, in a way, a good time to move on...move forward."

Josy said, "That would have been a good time to tell me about all this."

"You're right, but Harry, your dad; you know how he adored you. He couldn't face you being disappointed in him. Yes, that was wrong and I supposed cowardly of him. It's just he worshiped the ground you walked on. You were his princess."

Josy moved to the window seat; Sarah and Mama H. followed. They all sat for a while looking out the window. Josy finally said, "That was a big secret to keep from me all these years. And no one in town ever said anything about it? Mama H., did you ever hear about this?" Mama H. shook her head 'no'.

Sarah interjected, "Ellie would have none of that. She made George and Harry and I promise to never to say a word. As far as the town goes, only the sheriff and we knew what caused the accident. No one else needed to. The paper had few details about the cause of the accident. It was "under investigation" was all that was ever told to the public. And besides, the story the whole town focused on, and rightly so, was the loss..." Again Sarah paused... "Of this beautiful little girl." Sarah stared out the window holding back tears. She watched a robin fly across the street and land on the power lines. A possible mate joined her and they danced on that thin line as if it was the largest dance floor ever.

Sarah let out a big sigh, then she turned and looked at Josy, "I remember...now...I remember why they went for a drive...They went to get beef on weck; just going out to dinner"…another long sigh… "when they were coming home the brake line gave out as they were coming down the hill toward the railroad tracks. There was a train going through the intersection. George had no choice but to ditch the car. When they hit the embankment little Laney got thrown and..." Sarah stopped and started to cry. Mama H. reached over to hold her hand. Sarah regained her composure and finished, "You see her head hit the roof of the car. Her little neck just snapped. It was 1959...no seat belts."

Again, the three women just stared out the window for a long time as the spring was bringing new life to the neighborhood.

6

THE PINTO AND GREG

Life was moving on as Josy continued working at the D.M.V. and Sarah made dinner most nights for her. She also got some counseling from a therapist Mama H. knew. In those sessions she learned that when a child is traumatized, that in some ways they get stuck at that age in their mental/social development. It made sense that the fear of that night stayed with her and that it had stunted her growth in a sense.

I'm still fourteen in many ways. She realized one morning as she drank her coffee looking out her apartment window. It wasn't a window seat like at her mom's house but is was a garden window with an assortment of cacti, violets and other flowers. From there she could see the colorful fields of the farmlands that surrounded the village. Summers' corn crops were growing well, hay fields were getting ready for a first cutting, and the sun was high in the vast blue sky.

Something had changed for Josy. She wasn't as down on her job these days. She started looking at the folks coming in to get plates or licenses differently, not as the 'next' person to deal with, but as an opportunity to help someone with their day and maybe make it a little easier and nicer. Looking at each person as an opportunity made her job more fun. More like an adventure. That is, as long as she could keep up that mindset, which was not always easy. Sitting there, thinking about her job she mused, *Some customers can be…well, I'll leave that word out.* But she kept working at keeping a good attitude. She remembered pumping gas for folks when she was so young. They were always surprised a little girl could do that. It gave her a good feeling to get compliments and tips from them as she checked the oil and washed their windshields.

One evening while washing dinner dishes with Sarah, Josy said, "You know Mom, I miss the old gas station sometimes."

"Really?" Sarah replied."

"Yes, I do remember all the good times there. I really enjoyed meeting people and pumping their gas, checking their oil and all. It made me feel good. It wasn't rocket science, but it was necessary and I liked it. I guess, it took all these years for me to realize that."

"Well, I miss it too. I loved seeing you out there in all the seasons. I could see your joy in helping people. That's why I always had hot chocolate on for you in the winter and iced tea in the summer. You deserved a treat after being out there in the cold and the heat. Your Dad and I were always so proud of you, working so hard."

"Well, I was so proud of you…after all you were the one facing down cancer. I was glad I could do something, anything to help."

Sarah then said with a sigh "Those were the good times."

Josy picked up on that comment, and asked, "How are you doing Mom? I'm here most every night for dinner but we have not talked much about everything."

"O my dear, it's okay. One day at a time, you know. You're going through it too."

"Oh yeah, I forgot," Josy interjected, "I got the logbook back to Mr. Walker. I made copies of the pages with Dad's entries and I have them in the Pinto. I keep forgetting to bring them in."

"Bring them in and we'll put them with the photos and other funeral papers for now," Sarah said.

Josy went out to get them and looked around at the summer evening. It was still very light outside. The trees let the sun's rays dance in their leaves…sparkling away in joy. The sunset made the paint on her wagon seem new again. It was that late 70's orange, a bit dull now, but with the sun hitting it, the paint seemed to return to its original color. Josy suddenly had a thought. She needed to make that coffee date with Greg. She was sure he would not call, he was always too shy. She would have gone on a date with him in high school but he never asked. She finally gave up on him ever asking. So she went out with the first guy who did ask, and of course he turned out to be, well, the guy who had only one thing on his mind. Josy shook her head at that thought and decided she would call Greg.

Back in the house she said to her mom, "You know, Mom, I bought that old Pinto 2 years out of high school with your help and Dad's help. Did I ever thank you for that? I can't remember doing that."

Sarah thought a second and replied, "I'm sure you did. And you are thankful now, so it's all good."

"So, is that the way it works with you Mom? Like a time warp? Thankful now counts for being thankful back then?"

"Hey, that is not a bad saying. Thankful now, counts for being thankful then."

"You're too good to me Mom," Josy said as she put her arm around her. "Here are the pages, I will put them in that box that has been sitting there for the last 6 months."

"I know, I know, I am just not ready to do anything with it all yet."

"O, Mom, I know. I was just joking. After all, I'm a bigger procrastinator than you, and besides as Mama H. says, 'Grief has no timetable,'" Josy put the papers in the box. She looked back at her mom, who was just staring. "Mom, are you okay?" Josy asked.

"Oh, it just hits me...sometimes...I go into the bedroom to ask your father a question...and he's not there. Or I look at you...like right now, and see his eyes. He had such eyes." Sarah started to tear up, so Josy gave her a hug and spun her in a slow loving dance. "We are in this together," she said. And, as they turned, Josy spied the video tape in the box.

"Mom, you know next week, will be 6 months…since…we should watch that video tape again. Maybe we could invite Mama H. over too. I think it would be good for us to see it. The funeral home did such a nice job."

"Okay, if you think so, I am game." Sarah sat down on the window seat.

"Yeah? Well, then, I will call Mama H. and I will do the cooking."

"Well," her mom paused, "I would be glad to make dinner honey."

"Uhh," Josy looked at her mom... "Are you saying I can't cook?"

Sarah replied with a smirk, "You were always better with a wrench in your hand than a spatula, dear."

Josy joined her mom on the window seat. "Okay, okay. Speaking of that, wrenches that is...I have had an idea. I will run it by you and Mama H. when we get together."

"Sounds interesting, what is it?"

"I need to run it by a friend first. I will know more next week."

Greg agreed to a coffee date and Josy offered to drive up on her day off. After all, a drive to the lake in summer was a treat. As they sat out on the patio at the restaurant, Josy's thoughts turned to that night she spent in the parking lot. It was a terrible night that gave way to a joyous morning. She sighed in contentment as she sipped her coffee and eyed her old friend. Greg finally asked how she and her mom were doing.

"We are doing better, at least I am, I think," Josy said. "It is not simple...as you know...with your sister's passing."

"It is...no easy thing." Greg said as he stared at his coffee, shaking his head. He thought for a moment, looked at Josy as she watched a fisherman casting from shore, and then added, "But sometimes even bad things can bring about good things."

Josy looked at him with obvious questions on her mind. Greg said, "Maybe someday I will tell you. But remember, you asked me here for a reason...what is it?"

"I asked you to meet me because I want to run an idea by you."

"And what is your idea, And why would you want my opinion?"

"Well," you know that old Pinto of mine. I thought I would like to restore it. You know, fix it up and give it a new paint job."

Greg thought a moment and said, "You know, I have the garage of course, and I have a friend who paints cars. You know what? He could get that original color, that orange. And we could give that engine a real going over too. We could shave the head, do a 3 angle valve job, port the intake manifold and exhaust, change the degree of the cam... and you should be able to wind that out close to 9000 rpms with no problem."

"Woah!" Josy jumped in, "Run that one by me again, a little slower... it's been a long time since I was on the inside of an engine, you know."

"Sorry, it's just that I have been thinking about restorations for a while. I would like to expand my business. And I have been helping some of my 'wrench head' friends with engines. And ever since that day in April, I have been thinking about you...your car I mean...and so...I know what I would like to do...but...what do you think?"

Josy smiled, "I like it! And you know, we could upgrade the tranny and differential too. Stiffen up the suspension, and put some wide rubber on it with some nice mags. I think I'm getting excited."

"I am too," said Greg with a laugh, "It'll be like old times at BOCES."

"I always liked working with you," Josy replied.

"Me too," said Greg, "I mean, I liked working with you too."

The two of them took sips of coffee and looked out over the lake. There were sailboats with their sails wide open skimming across the water and in the foreground sea gulls finding their thermals and floating along freely. Josy thought to herself, *Today is a good day...and a great painting too.* And then she asked Greg, "So tell me, how did you end up here by the lake?"

Greg took another sip of his coffee and answered, "Well, let me see... after graduation I worked for a few years at Johansson's Chevrolet. It was there that I went to school for GM Mechanical training. It really helped me and I moved up in the ranks. After a while I just wanted to be my own boss. It can be hard when you are just a number, if you know what I mean...Johansson is a big company...lots of employees. So I began looking around...literally. I drove all over looking at the garages and auto dealerships. One day, five years ago...it was after my sister's death...I was here in town and stopped in this very restaurant. I got talking with some guys and found out that the owner of the garage around the corner was looking to retire. So, I bought in as a partner and eventually bought him out."

Josy asked, "How did you afford that? If I may ask."

"My parents, God bless them, took out a home equity loan to give me the buy-in share and then when I was ready the next year, the bank gave me a loan for the rest."

"That was very kind of your parents. How are they doing?"

"Good, they still live back in town, same house as always. I only get to see them on holidays lately, I'm so busy. But they also come up here for a lunch or dinner. It's not a bad place to visit."

"You're right about that my friend."

"Yeah, my parents always have been there for me, even though there were tough times. My mom had trouble with depression, and it wasn't easy for many years. It was hidden back then...you know how things were...always kept in the family."

"Yes I know, trust me I know."

Greg looked at her with a questioning expression.

"Someday I will tell you all about it."

"Hey, that was my line. Are you making fun of me?"

Josy chuckled. "It just keeps things interesting, don't you think? It just gives us more to talk about later." Greg gave her a smile and took another sip.

They continued to look out over the lake, where a huge ship was passing slowly along the horizon. Josy asked Greg, "So, do you have friends here?"

"Well, a few. No girlfriends if that's what you mean...I am still shy when it comes to that."

"You know," Josy said, "I was always waiting for you to ask me out back in high school." Greg was a bit startled by that statement. "I... aah I..." Josy jumped in. "It's okay...that was then, this is now. I didn't mean to put you on the spot."

Greg motioned for the waiter for more coffee."I was...scared...to ask you out. You, well...you were, I thought, out of my league."

Josy laughed a little and replied, "Me? Really? I never thought of myself as being out of anyone's league."

"Well, I always thought you were, beautiful." Greg blushed a little while saying it. "I'm in my thirties and I still get like a high school kid around you," he said with a laugh.

"It's okay, I am the same."

Coffee was poured as the two eyed each other. They could see a connection growing.

"So, did your mom get the help she needed?" Josy asked.

"Yes, she did, although the medications did not always work. It's so hard to get them right. Each person is different and it takes time. It wasn't easy, and there were many bumps in the road as they say. Without my family's support and her therapist...she would probably be...well...I don't like to think about it, especially with my sister Anne's death. When she got diagnosed with leukemia, I think that's when my mom really came to grips with her need for professional help. It was her

63

daughter and she knew she needed to be there for Anne with the best positive attitude she could muster. She went to therapy the next week and has never stopped."

"That must have been hard on you,"

Greg took a deep sigh. "Yes, but it was my mom. And my sister, God bless her soul, was a champion through it all. She never gave up hope on herself or my mom. And, now, to see my mom on an even keel...has been worth every second of the hard times."

They both looked once more out over the lake. It was time to pay the check and part company, but Greg said he would give Josy a call the next week and talk some more.

"So, you will call me?" Josy asked with a smile.

"Yes," said Greg... "Yes, I definitely will." They both laughed as they parted.

He called on a Thursday night, late. Josy picked up the phone and they talked for a bit and then Greg asked a question. "Now about the Pinto...How will you pay for this, Josy? It won't be cheap, even doing the engine work ourselves. I don't mean to be a dream killer, but it is something you need to consider."

Josy, laughed, "You know, my dream car has always been a Shelby... well I have scrimped and saved for what seems forever and I have a good sum to spend. But I've decided that I really don't want to let go of my old Pinto. So forget the Shelby...for now...I'll put the money into the wagon. Let's figure out the cost of this and see where we land and get together again soon."

Greg said, "Yes let's do that. Do you want me to drive down this time?"

Josy said, "Sure."

So they met at Humphries the following week for lunch. Greg brought estimates of costs and parts catalogues, paint swatches and photos of interior restorations. They sat for hours looking, talking and dreaming. Greg said that he would get a final plan together with all the costs and they could get together again to look it over.

Driving back home Josy was excited…she patted the dash board of her car and talked to it. "I know I have called you a few choice names lately, but really, for the most part, you've been a good car all these years and we're going to give you a new life. I can't wait to make you shine again." She thought of the old days with Greg and her working side by side. Passing wrenches and talking cars. They never got together back then, but, she thought. *Maybe someday…soon…we'll go on a real date…the three of us. Three on a date is normally a crowd, but when your third is a wagon…well…*Josy laughed out loud and blushed at her sudden reversion to teenage thinking.

A few weeks had passed and she and Greg had finalized a plan for the Pinto's restoration. Sarah thought this was a great idea and also liked that Josy was seeing a guy that she could easily relate to. "It seems like you will have a lot of fun doing this with Greg," she said to Josy one Saturday morning.

"We will, I'm sure of it, I always liked Greg. We think alike, at least when it comes to cars. I hope to find out what else we have in common."

Sarah smiled as she put the scrambled eggs on the table. "Thanks for coming over for breakfast."

"And thank you for the breakfast Mom…and…so, I have asked Mama H. to come for a cookout and she has agreed to next Sunday afternoon. I will clean up the grill and get some charcoal."

"Well, I never did the grillin', that was your dads department…do you think you can manage to burn some dogs and burgers?"

"Sure Mom, I can burn anything!"

They laughed at that comment and poured some coffee. "You know Mom," Josy said, "Ever since you told me about what happened back in '59, things are better for me. I mean, I just feel better about life, my work and I am definitely excited about the Pinto."

"And Greg too?"

"Well, yes, Mom. I don't know where that is going but even if it is just friendship, it's one I look forward to. It's funny, I have more in common with Greg than any of my girlfriends. I guess I have always been a Tomboy."

Sarah said, "What does that mean, anyway, Tomboy? I believe God gives us all talents, gifts and yearnings. It doesn't matter if they fit into some societal norm. Those rules are for scaredy cats."

"Wow! That's quite a radical statement for an old conservative lady."

"Hey! You're only as old as you allow your thinking to get. I spent too many years trying to avoid the past, only to keep running into it.

I had to face it and then let it go. Like you said. Ever since the truth of that day came out of my mouth, I feel…young! And my old judgements and rules are just that, old. You have to move with the Spirit; and that Wind blows into new places, brooding and waiting to create something amazing."

"Preach it Mom!" said Josy, with a laugh.

Her mom continued, "You know, Josy, whatever you were as a child and now as a woman is a gift to me. You were a gift to your father and to everyone you have been around." Josy just took that comment in like a breath of fresh air. Normally she would brush off such compliments, but this morning she just let the love pouring from her moms' words warm her heart like a wool scarf in a cold winter wind.

"Thanks Mom. I appreciate that. You sound like Mama H. and my counselor."

"Well, truth is not the monopoly of one person, it is shared evenly throughout the world with those who are humble and open to it."

Josy was not used to her mom being so outspoken unless she was in her mother lion mode. Many a time during her growing up years, her mom would fiercely defend her as she went through various struggles. But then, once things were resolved, she would return to her quiet self. These days she was like an unleashed puppy running free. It was beautiful. Josy got up to put her plate in the sink and gave her mom a hug from behind. "I love you so much, Mom," she said. Sarah returned the sentiment and they both cleaned up the table.

The next week, Josy spent more time with Greg going over details of the Pinto's restoration. While they were talking, Greg said, "Josy, the way you talk about the interior and exterior work, well...you should do this...at least you might want to think about doing it more...like for others."

Josy looked at him and thought for a moment. "You know I have always wanted to be in some kind of auto design. You really think I could do this and make a living?"

"Absolutely, and there is a market for detailing and restorations, and good money in it. As I said before, I have been wanting to branch out into it but I just don't have the time...and I haven't met the right person to head it up for me. Well, until you came back into my life. What do you think? You want to take a chance on me and you?...in business together...I mean...umm...," he looked down at his oil stained shoes... "I mean, I wouldn't mind if the 'you and me' meant something more...I don't mean to be...well I just don't want to assume anything."

Josy looked out his garage window as convertible Mustangs, Corvettes and other cars passed by on the way to the beaches of Ontario. She smiled and said, "You and me...and the Pinto makes three." She laughed and said, "It's an inside joke." And then blushed, laughing even more.

"What's so funny?"

"Someday, maybe, I will tell you."

"Oh, not that again," Greg laughed.

Josy laughed too and then said, "Anyway, I am also open to whatever this is between us and whatever it may become."

And then, Greg got a call for a tow job. They hugged and parted, both filled with many thoughts of a future together in more ways than just business.

The day of the cookout came and Mama H. brought her famous strawberry glaze pie. Sarah made her potato salad and Josy did the grillin'. They sat at the picnic table, ate, drank and talked 'till sunset. After cleaning up they went inside to have dessert. Josy told Mama H. and Sarah about the plans and dreams she and Greg talked about.

Mama H. said, "I'm glad you have dreams....You can't create anything without dreaming about it first."

Sarah said, "Yes, like what it says in Genesis, 'The Spirit, the Holy Wind was brooding over the face of the deep.' And then…God created."

Mama H. chimed in… "See, even God dreamed about creation first."

"Okay, you two, you're ganging up on me with all this religious profundity."

Mama H. suddenly got more serious, and said softly, "Religion? No not religion…it is faith…religion is of human origin, but faith? That is of the Divine. Never confuse the two."

Sarah added, "Amen!"

"Okay," said Josy with some sarcasm in her voice, as she escaped to the window seat with her pie and camomile tea.

Sarah and Mama H. joined her and then Mama H. asked, "I am

dying to hear about Lacey MacClean. I am sorry for jumping the gun and asking, after I said you could tell me, when and if you ever wanted. But I am human...and curious. Who is this super woman you dreamed up?"

Josy just looked at her with eyes that said it plainly.

"Oh no!" Said Mama H., "I assumed you told your mom."

Sarah asked, "Told me what?"

Josy was a bit taken aback but as she looked out the window at the sunset, it reminded her of the sunrise just a few months earlier. She remembered the scents of spring and the feeling of hope as she saw the sky painting of that day.

"Well, my big little secret's out now to you both, well...and the therapist of course. And I am glad, because I have not thought of Lacey in a while. Maybe I have outgrown my childish fantasies."

Sarah asked, "What are you talking about, dear?"

"You see Mom, I have been dreaming of this Scottish woman, Lacey MacClean...she is my, or was my, alter ego. She's an F1 driver for McClaren"

Sarah gasped. "F1! Not NASCAR?"

Josy laughed, "Yeah, I know, but she also has a ride on the dirt track circuit in the off season. Anyway, I have fantasized about being like her... you know; all confident, with it, accomplished, and a cool name..."

At that, Josy stopped. And just looked out the window, thinking of her dad...and realizing that her name, chosen by her parents out of love for family meant something more than she ever appreciated. Their ancestors were proud people too. Her name, Josephine, was her great grandmother's who was beloved in the community back in Canada. Josy sighed and said, "It doesn't matter anyway."

Mama H. said, "I think it does matter, at least a little, because, as you dream, you may become. Without a dream, who are we? Without a dream, a vision, even sometimes a fantasy, there can be no creativity."

Sarah said, "You know...Harry and I had a dream. It was a simple one...to raise a child to be a beautiful person. And look at you my dear, you have been such a help to me. Remember when I was sick? You had to start working at such a young age, and you were so good at it...you literally increased our business. It was like some folks who come across lemonade stands, they buy because there is a child who is just trying to earn a little spending money...and sometimes they might be trying to earn money to help buy food for the table. People from town saw you out there and stopped to get gas just because they knew I was sick and you were doing your best to help. And of course, you endured the rage of George Abernathy and all that entailed. Josy, you had the courage to be the only girl to take the auto course in school. And I could go on, but know this. You are a strong woman and don't ever forget it, you're as good as any Lacey...whoever she is."

Mama H. agreed wholeheartedly and then said, "Well, it's getting late and I should go." She said her goodbyes and Sarah and Josy both thanked her again for all she had done for them over the last 6 months. After Mama H. left, Josy and Sarah realized they forgot about the video.

Kevin Bailey

"Is it too late to watch the tape, Mom?"

"I am game if you are."

So Josy put the video tape in the new VCR. They watched the video, laughed and cried together arm in arm on the sofa.

7

DRIVING INTO THE SUNRISE

Over the next few months, there was a lot to do. First of all finding a cheap winter rat for Josy to drive while the Pinto was being taken apart. So Josy and Greg went down to the car auction in Manheim, PA and found a '85 Nova with only 45,000 miles. They towed it back to New York. Greg pulled into Bingham's restaurant for a cream puff and coffee on the way.

"Now I know why your Dad liked this place," Greg said.

"We always looked forward to these treats when he came home. Thank you for bringing me down here and towing my new car back for me."

"It's no problem, I am happy to do it. I like spending more time with you, and…um…listen, one of these Saturdays after working on the car, can we go out for dinner and a movie or something?"

"Yes, I would like that," Josy said as they headed out the door.

The fall colors were in full bloom in the southern tier, and the drive back up Route 81 was beautiful. As they drove along, Greg said, "I think we can have the Pinto ready by next spring...maybe we should shoot for your birthday...St. Patty's Day...that would be a nice present to yourself."

"That would be really nice. I think that is a plan. Let's work hard to make that happen. Okay?"

"Yes...definitely."

As the orange colors of fall were giving way to the browns and whites of winter, the orange paint was going on the Pinto's fenders and panels. Things were shaping up nicely with the body work, but the engine was proving to be more of a hassle. Finding parts and doing all the work was slow. That was okay, though, because they wanted the restoration to be perfect. Then, there was a lot of rust on the underside of the wagon to deal with. A lot of work went into cleaning it up and making it solid again. But they were having fun even with the extra work. Every weekend they were getting to know each other a little better. And the idea of going into business together progressed as well.

One day over coffee Greg said, "I have been thinking, here is a name for the restoration business...'Josy's Details'...or maybe 'Details... Details'...what do you think?"

"I like them both, but you know, Greg, it could just be part of your business. No need for a separate name."

"Well, I think it needs to be set apart in a way so that people notice and it has a good ring to it. So if I have your permission, I will get a sign made. Which one do you like?"

"Ummm…I kinda like the second," Josy said. "But I think I should start part time and still work until it is sustainable, before you make an investment in a sign."

"Absolutely," Greg agreed. "We can start slow and work up to it."

Josy thought to herself, *Kinda like our relationship*. She smiled at Greg and nodded okay.

As the months of winter passed, the first year anniversary of her dad's death came around. Josy and Sarah went to the grave. There was a bitter winter wind that day as they stood there talking to Harry, but they did not feel the cold. They focused on the shared love they had for this man, this husband, father and friend.

Later, having coffee and sitting at the window seat, Josy remembered that day a year ago. "Mom, do you remember Mr. Abernathy was at the ER that day last year. I saw him in the hallway. Did you?"

Sarah replied, "No…wait…George was there? I guess I was too focused on your dad to see much else."

"Yeah, I get that, Mom, but he was there, and I have to say, I was, well…frozen, until you stepped in front of me."

"Frozen?"

"Yes, frozen with fear. It was like I was right back at the station that night. I mean, it's all good now…well it's better and getting better each day…that's my new phrase these days…and it's true."

"Wow, that must have been…I don't know…hard for you. I'm so

sorry I don't remember seeing him. But I do know that I heard that he had suffered a stroke. I don't think he is in his home anymore. I heard he was in the nursing home."

Josy thought about that and said, "I wonder if I should see him?"

"See him?" Do you think that is wise. I mean it's been a long time and...well...I don't know...do you really want to?"

Josy looked out the window...the snow was blowing across the lawn and piling up on the East fence. "I feel I need to move forward Mom, and I think that a visit to Mr. Abernathy may be what allows me to do so."

Sarah said, "You have come so far...do you really feel the need?"

"Well, seeing him…well...I think I just need to Mom."

"Okay then, Eleanor can get you in to see him, I'm sure."

"Yes, I will call her. Maybe not right away, but soon, I think," Josy said as she got up to get another cup of coffee. "You want another cup, Mom?"

"Not right now, dear, but thank you anyway,"

The new year came and time was flying as Greg and Josy worked hard to complete the Pinto project in time for St. Patrick's Day. They did go out for dinner and a movie but they were so focused on the car that they whispered about it throughout the movie making a few people near them a bit annoyed. But they were like teenagers giggling at the 'Shushes'...which made the people even more annoyed. Finally, they tried to focus on the movie, for the sake of the other moviegoers. Afterwards, they walked down the street and agreed to not go to a movie again until the car was done.

One day under the Pinto Greg said, "You know, this Pinto is going to move. A few more modifications and we could try it out on the eighth mile...what do you think?"

"Race it?"

"Well, I know you want to go fast. And hey, why not give it a try."

"I will need some training, but...ahh...I don't know."

"Hey come on, don't limit yourself...and I could give it a go too,"

"Maybe." Josy replied.

The day they finally finished the engine, and there wasn't a single extra bolt to be found...they celebrated. An extra bolt could mean trouble...almost as bad as an empty bolt hole, which could mean the bolt was in the engine...not good. But when they fired it up...it ran smoothly. They breathed a sigh of relief and went out to dinner with the painter and Greg's employees. Everyone had a part in rebuilding the car in one way or another. Soon the engine would be back in the car and they would be finishing the interior and giving it all the final touches. Josy and Greg were so excited they hugged and gave each other a kiss. Their first...and Josy thought...*That is not our only kiss...I hope.*

St. Patrick's Day arrived and Greg was bringing the Pinto down from the lake as the house party was prepared by Sarah and Mama H.

Josy, standing there, asked, "Can I help?"

"No, no, you go to the diner for a coffee while we get the house ready," Sarah said.

Josy tried to just start helping out, but was told forcefully to "Get out!"...Mama H. was trying to do her best impression of the *Terminator*.

Josy replied in kind, "I'll be back!"

As Josy drove to the diner, she thought, *This is going to be a big day.* Frank brought her a coffee as she sat at the diner counter. Josy sipped away and had time to think over some things, but mostly about her recent visit to Mr. Abernathy.

It was in late February and she walked into his room behind Mama H., who brought Josy up to speed on his condition. "Now, George doesn't talk much. It's still hard for him to form words, but he will understand what you are saying. He doesn't look at much but mostly just stares out his window. So don't expect much interaction. Just say what you want to...or don't say anything...just be present in any case. I will be just in the hall if you need me."

Josy thanked her and sat down next to Mr. Abernathy. She was shaking a little. She had never got this close to the man who was the 'monster' that terrible night. She did not know what to say. They sat there in silence for a while.

Finally, Josy got up and faced him as best she could. She said, "Mr. Abernathy, you may not recognize me...it's been so many years...I am Josy...um...I am Josephine Daudry and I am here because after all these years I was finally told of what happened to your little girl...Laney. I never knew. My parents did not tell me. I only found out last year when Dad died."

Josy looked out the window at that point and suddenly wondered if he knew it was her dad in the ER that day. *Was Mr. Abernathy happy to see my dad on a gurney...did he feel my dad got what he thought he deserved?* She shook her head of those negative thoughts and then continued.

"I am so sorry...for what happened. And I understand now why you were so sad. I was very scared of you for many years. But I am okay now and, Mr. Abernathy; I forgive you. And I hope that you have found some peace, I hope you have been able to forgive my dad's mistake. It made me feel pretty bad, that in a way, it was me who caused all this. I know I am not responsible and I know my dad's intentions were only to save me. And believe me, I know he was torn up for years about it... right up until his last year.

"Anyway I just wanted to say that I know my mom prays for you and if you know Mama...I mean Mrs. Humphries, well she can...maybe help you find comfort and peace. She was there and is still there for my mom and I in our loss of Dad."

Josy could not think of anything else to say, so she sat back down and looked out the window for a few more minutes. Then she got up and said, "I need to go." Josy looked at Mr. Abernathy as he just stared out the window. After a few moments she turned, touched his shoulder and walked out the door to Mama H.

She did not see George, as he looked down from the window at a photo of Ellie, Laney and himself from 1958. He stared at the picture frame...it was a window into past beauty...he lived in his memories of those happy days. As he stared at it...a tear ran down his cheek.

Coming out of the memory of that visit, Josy sat there at the counter on her second cup of coffee. Frank said, "Hey Josy, we're closing in a bit. Better get going to your party."

"You're right." Josy said as she tried to leave money for the coffee.

"Happy Birthday," Frank pushed her money back to her.

"Thanks Frankie," she said as she headed for the door. "See you there?".

"Absolutely!" Frank responded.

It was a windy March day...there were big parades in the cities...green beer and fun. But Josy knew that was the American way of celebrating this day. In Ireland it was more of a somber holiday commemorating the patron saint. She thought about this being her second birthday without her dad and it seemed that a somber celebration might be more appropriate. She thought, *St. Patrick and other famous people have hundreds if not thousands of years of remembrances...such a long time to let grieving give way to celebration. It's not fair that most of us only have a generation or two before we are completely forgotten. We need to tell our stories...keep our loved ones' memories honored.*

Then, she wondered what her mom, Mama H., and Greg had planned. As she pulled onto her mom's street...she found out. There were cars parked up and down the street...and only one spot was left in the driveway. Greg was outside waiting for her to pull in.

He acted like a valet...stopping her and opening her door. She got out to his outstretched hand and he said in a feigned Irish accent, "I'll be parking your car, me lass."

She graciously curtsied back and said, "Why thank you me good man," in her best accent.

As they walked through the front door, the house was packed with family, friends, villagers and people she wasn't sure she knew. Everyone yelled, "Happy Birthday, Josy!" And the party was on...it was not a somber celebration...and Josy didn't mind. After everyone had some food, Greg got up and announced that her present was in the back yard.

"How many of us make our own birthday presents?" Then he yelled, "Josephine Daudry does!"

Everyone cheered, and, being led by Josy, they paraded out to the yard. And there it was. The Pinto in all its glory, shining in the sunset. The orange paint job gleaming, the mags shining...the interior...perfect.

Greg had rigged up lights to shine up from below as well. It was a showcase. And there was a table full of pitchers of...you guessed it...green beer, with a picture of her Dad. They all toasted to Josy and the car. Josy looked at her mom and the two of them toasted to Harry, lifting their glasses to the heavens. It was a good day and a great sky.

Later on Josy and Greg sat on the window seat looking out at the clear night sky. Stars were shimmering in the deep navy expanse.

Greg thought out loud..."Tomorrow is going to be a sunny day."

"I know what you're thinking," Josy was smiling as she said, "Yes, we should take the Pinto for her first drive."

We can, maybe let her wind out a bit?"

"Sounds like a plan," Josy agreed.

Greg stayed over that night along with Sarah's nieces, her brother, and his wife. They all camped out wherever they could. Josy awoke early and came down stairs and just sat on the step looking over the 'sleeping beauties' for a bit. She then tiptoed to the kitchen where she found her mom.

"Thank you so much for the party Mom,"

Sarah gave her a hug and said, "You are very welcome my dear."

They sat at the table and talked in whispers about many things.

Sarah said, "The good Lord has answered my prayers for you, my girl."

"I kinda see that. And I like the way things are going. I don't know what the future holds, but I am ready to face it...because I know I am not alone."

"Certainly not," Sarah mused as she spied Greg shuffling toward them.

Later that morning, Josy and Greg got into the Pinto and fired it up. It sounded so good. Josy revved the engine, then slowly let out the clutch to pull out of the back yard. She then drove down through the village, past the diner, and swung around by St. David's, then, finally past the old garage"

Greg said, "Maybe someday...you could buy that back."

Josy thought to herself, *Why not?*

She just gave Greg a smile as they turned north toward the lake. She came to a stop sign at the four corners about a half mile out of town and Greg said, "Let's see what she's got."

Josy revved it up and then let the car go...she wound it out with her foot to the floor. She made 100 mph in third gear and then shut it down. Greg and her both let out joyous screams as the sheriff's siren followed them to the curb.

The young deputy got to the driver's side window and acted professionally asking for her license and registration. He then broke down in laughter..."O Josy...I knew you wouldn't be able to help yourself...I was waiting for you...what took you so long?"

They all laughed at that and Josy asked, "Did you get enough to eat last night?"

"O yeah," he replied. "Now, I'm letting you off with a warning... Ma'am...and try to keep it under 85...okay?"

They laughed again and he gave Greg a slight salute.

As the deputy drove away, Josy turned to Greg and asked, "Did you arrange that...Greg?"

"I can neither confirm or deny that, Ma'am."

Josy smiled as they pulled away...slowly...the sky through the windshield beckoning them northward. Josy said, "I love the sky...you know?"

"I do too. That's one reason I love living on the lake."

They picked up speed. Then Josy had a now familiar thought... *Greg and me and the Pinto make three...* and then, she smiled even wider.

Josy D., is free. Somewhere, in whatever reality she may be...Lacey MacClean is thinking... *Josephine Daudry...now that's a good name.*

The End

Printed in the United States
by Baker & Taylor Publisher Services